Dougal
and the Blue Cat

Dougal
and the Blue Cat

ERIC THOMPSON

From an original film by Serge Danot

BLOOMSBURY

First published in 1999

The publishers would like to thank Amanda Pappin for providing a video of the film, and
Eric Thompson's family for providing the original hand-written manuscript.

Bloomsbury Publishing Plc, 38 Soho Square, London, W1V 5DF

A CIP catalogue record for this book is available from the British Library

ISBN 0 7475 4427 1

10 9 8 7 6 5 4 3 2 1

Typeset by Hewer Text
Printed in Great Britain by Clays Limited

Introduction by Bruce Robinson

My first year at Drama School ended in near disaster. I was hauled in by the theatrical authorities to be informed that I suffered from a substantial disability in terms of my aspirations. It wasn't just the lisp, stoop, and sweating. They could handle that. What they couldn't deal with was the almost comprehensive lack of talent. It was explained that what might have gone down tits in the arts columns of the *Isle Of Thanet Gazette*, wasn't going down well here at all. 'You've had a very nasty year, haven't you?' I distinctly remember the conciliatory suggestion that there were all sorts of amateur-dramatic societies about the country that would satisfy my kind of requirement. (Apparently I wouldn't make a bad Hamlet in Herne Bay). Twenty-seven shillings and six pence would be the price of a one-way railway ticket that would destroy my life. This was 1964. And I was eighteen.

I can't remember whether I wept, but I do remember a certain intensity of pleading. In those days becoming an actor was everything I had ever wanted. The boss of Central School, Geroge Hall, was probably right, but also had a compassion the professional theatre doesn't readily allow. It is not the trade of angels. 'Anyway,' he said, 'listen, you can do a probationary term in the second year, but if things don't improve, I'm afraid it's the train.' I seized the straw, freaked myself sick with apprehension all that summer, and came back in September for the beginning of the second year. It was then that something astonishingly fortuitous happened. I met Eric Thompson.

Eric was a professional actor and friend of George's who had been persuaded to come to Central to direct us students in a play. Everything about Eric was immediately different to everything we had been accustomed to. He was carrying far too much energy for the usual thespianistic claptrap. You didn't even get a good morning. He was short, dark, and already getting on with it.

I sat there in the gloomy theatre, a perspiring mess of anxiety with a sibilant S. My arse was on the final line and there would be no negotiations.

It was my turn to read and I ground it out through hissing teeth. This went on for a minute or two before Eric interceded. 'What's the matter with you?' he said. 'What are you staring at the table for?' I forced my eyes from the text to reply. 'I'm sorry,' I said, 'I've got a bit of neck-tension.' He looked at me, Gauloise in his mouth, with an expression of benevolent contempt. 'Well then,' he snapped, 'get a bit of *back-tension*, and *sit the fuck up*.' It was an apocalyptic moment for me. It was the most pertinent and startling piece of theatrical instruction I had ever received, then, now, and for ever. I sat up. I got my head up and under Eric's direction managed to navigate the probation and acted my way into three full years at the Central School.

Years later, when I was just about scraping a quid as a professional actor myself, Eric cast me as Hibbert in *Journey's End*, a masterpiece of First World War histrionics that we played to enormous success at the Mermaid Theatre, London. I'd got a lot better by then, as I suppose had he. He was a magnificent director, and, although I couldn't have known it then, taught me so much about the craft of conspiring with actors, which I was to use when I too became a director, another long gang of years away. Working with Eric was the most important event in my theatrical career. Acting for him is among my most precious memories, so ingrained it re-emerged subliminally when I directed my first film, *Withnail and I*, long after he'd died. It is *Journey's End* that Marwood is reading in the disintegrating cottage at Penrith, and the lead in *Journey's End* that he abandons Withnail for at the close of the film.

I wish Eric could have seen *Withnail*. I know he would have liked it. Without learning from him, his precise and brilliant technique, I could never have directed it. It is a tragedy that Eric is gone. He was an extraordinary talent and shouldn't have shuffled it that young. But his spirit is still here. And when I don't know how to do it, I can still hear his voice . . .

On the opening night of *Journey's End* he gave me a book of poems by Siegfried Sassoon. I have it by me now, heartbreaking stuff of the First World War. There's one in there, untitled, that I can never read without thinking of Eric Thompson . . .

> Watch with me, inward solemn influence,
> Invisible, intangible, unkenned;
> Wind of the darkness that shall bear me hence;
> O life within my life, flame within flame,
> Who mak'st me one with song that has no end,
> And with that stillness whence my spirit came.

I don't know quite what it means. But as far as I'm concerned, it means something quite important about Eric. Anyway, it's good enough for me.

B.R. July 1999

Dougal

and the Blue Cat

Dawn broke in the Magic Garden. A cock crowed, birds sang and the CUCKOO *emerged from his clock, flapping his wings.*

CUCKOO: Dougal! If you don't get up I'll spit!

The CUCKOO *slammed his doors shut and the clock pendulum fell with a bump on to* DOUGAL's *sleeping form below.* DOUGAL *woke up with a start and rushed around in his nightcap, wondering what was going on.*

DOUGAL: What! What! What! What! Man the lifeboats! Ban the bomb! The dam's burst! Is me nightie on fire? Vote Conservative! Keep off the grass! What!? What!? What!? What!?

The CUCKOO *reappeared.*

CUCKOO: Don't get confused, my lovely.

DOUGAL *stood up in his bed and looked at the* CUCKOO.

DOUGAL: Oh, it's you! I might have known. I'll nail your doors together one of these days if you're not careful. Ooooh . . . You're so hearty!

The CUCKOO *disappeared again.* DOUGAL *remembered something.*

DOUGAL: I've just remembered. That was a very funny thing that happened last night. I must ask Zebedee about it.

Out popped the CUCKOO.

CUCKOO: Stop muttering and get up!

DOUGAL *shook his head and his nightcap fell off.*

DOUGAL: Uncouth creature! What I have to put up with . . .

DOUGAL *turned to a picture of* FLORENCE *hanging on the tree by his bed and gave it two big kisses.*

4

DOUGAL: Now Dougal, don't get sloppy!
Just have a cup of tea . . .

He jumped off the bed and went to fetch the teapot.

Funny about last night . . .

DOUGAL *drained the cup at a few gulps, then shook his head.*

Nectar!
That was *very* funny last
night . . .
Very funny . . . very *funny.*

The CUCKOO *reappeared once more.*

CUCKOO: Are you up yet?

DOUGAL *lost his temper.*

DOUGAL: I'll be up there in a minute!
Oooh . . . I hate a noisy clock.

As DOUGAL *wandered off into the garden a red train came puffing along towards him.* DOUGAL *met the train.*

DOUGAL: Ah! What a lucky chance. Could
                 you give me a lift?

TRAIN: (*Prissy*) Thet depends.

DOUGAL: Depends? What on? You're a
                 public service vehicle, aren't
                 you?

TRAIN: Thet may be, but it doesn't mean
                 ai can be taken advantage of . . .

DOUGAL: Oh, all right . . . don't get all
                 steamed up.

DOUGAL *jumped into the carriage, chuckling to
himself. The* TRAIN *slowly chugged along.*

                 This could lead anywhere.
                 (*Whisper*) It would be quicker to
                 walk but she gets very upset . . .

They crossed the big red bridge. DOUGAL *popped
his head out of the carriage wearing a number of
different hats: a Sombrero, a Berliner, a Cooli hat
and a floppy felt hat. He was proud of his
impressions.*

                 This is your captain speaking. In
                 four days we will be landing at

Watford Junction.
Or MADRID.
Or BERLIN
Or PEKING
Or BOURNEMOUTH

Did you like that? Oh . . . I'm so talented!

The TRAIN *began to puff in a panicky fashion, and the carriage rocked dangerously.*

TRAIN: Oh mai! Oh mai! Oh mai! Get off the line! Ai can't stop! Clear the tracks!

DOUGAL: What! What! What! Take care you steam-driven fool you! What do you think you're doing? You've got *me* on board. Oooh . . . I hate this . . . I hate it!

ERMINTRUDE *was standing right in the way. She lowered her head and horns menacingly. The train ground to a halt.* DOUGAL *jumped down from the carriage.*

ERMINTRUDE: Hallo, darlings . . .

DOUGAL: Madam, you've stopped my
                 train.

ERMINTRUDE: Oh – have I, dear boy?

DOUGAL: Yes, you have!

ERMINTRUDE: Oh, I create such chaos . . .
Chaos!

DOUGAL: You can say that again!

ERMINTRUDE: (*Fast*) It's just that I love
                 watching trains . . . All cows do
                 – it's a well known fact.
                 So if you're in a train and you
                 see some cows in a field – give
                 them a wave – they do so
                 appreciate it . . .
                 Goodbye, dear hearts.

ERMINTRUDE *waved her tail and continued on her
way. The train rolled its eyes.*
DOUGAL *jumped back on board.*

TRAIN: Oh mai! She does go on, that
                 one!

DOUGAL: What a way to run a railway.

They met BRIAN, *who was showing a pretty turn of speed.*

BRIAN: Come along, come along! Hurry up!

TRAIN: Beaten by a snail! Ai'll never be able to show me face in Crewe again.

DOUGAL: Snail! Come here at once.

BRIAN: Yes?

DOUGAL: What do you think you're doing?

BRIAN: Nothing, old matey. Just out for a stroll.

He zoomed round in a few circles.

Goodbye.

DOUGAL: Come out!

BRIAN: Yes!

DOUGAL: Listen. You've upset my transport and I'm in a hurry.

BRIAN: Oh, I'm sorry, old chum. I'm
                very sorry.

DOUGAL: No you're not!

BRIAN: Yes I am. Cross my heart. Funny
                the things which upset the
                railways these days . . .

They met DYLAN.

DOUGAL: Hallo, Rabbit! Hard at it I see?

DYLAN: Man, you're right. I'm watching
                those crazy mushrooms grow.
                It's . . . like . . . very tiring.
                Like . . . exhausting.

He collapsed in a heap.

DOUGAL: You know, he's doing the rabbit
                image no good at all.

MR MACHENRY *came up on his bicycle.*

MACHENRY: (*Irish*) Good morning. It's a
                lovely day, isn't it?

DOUGAL: I don't wish to appear churlish,
                Mr MacHenry, but I am in
                rather a hurry.

MACHENRY: Oh well, don't let me detrain
               you then. I've got things to do.
               Flowers to grow, spuds to pull
               and lots of things horticultural
               to attend to . . . Yes indeed and
               begorrah!

DOUGAL: Yes indeed and begorrah? He's
               off his head. I've always thought
               all that mulching was dangerous.

The TRAIN *rolled its eyes a few times.*

DOUGAL: What now?

TRAIN: Oh mai!

DOUGAL: Got your sleepers in a twist,
               have you?

TRAIN: Look over there.

ZEBEDEE *was conducting a chorus line of pretty
French lollipops.*

DOUGAL: Er . . .

ZEBEDEE: Don't interrupt, please.

LOLLIPOP: Oh, 'e's joli . . .

11

TRAIN: Perhaps you gals would like to come for a ride? I'm going to Middlesboro'

Great excitement as the LOLLIPOPs *boarded the train.*

LOLLIPOP: Oh, you're *all* so joli 'ere!

ZEBEDEE: What a charming lot. French, you know.

DOUGAL: (*Sinister*) Yes, they look absolutely delicious . . . I've got something to ask you.

ZEBEDEE: Ask away. Ask away. Any little problems you've got – you can always bring them to me. You know what I'm like, always ready to help. Me and my magic moustache. Just ask . . . go on . . . ask. Just ask. Ask away. Any little problems and I'll do my best to solve them. Don't worry about troubling me – just *ask*.

DOUGAL: Well I'm *very* glad we've established *that* because there *is*

a little problem I'd like to discuss.
Are you listening?
Well, it's about last night.

ZEBEDEE: Yes? Last night?

DOUGAL: I was asleep last night when something happened . . .
You see, I'd gone to bed early with a cup of cocoa and a biccy because I'd had rather a tiring day what with one thing and another. You know how it is. And I was fast asleep and dreaming a lovely dream about getting me Knighthood at the palace.
A dream I often have, I don't know why . . .
When suddenly – I woke up. I was wide awake . . . why?
Was my hot water bottle leaking? No. So, what was I doing *awake* when I should have been asleep and dreaming . . . if you see what I mean?
What had woken me up?
Now I don't often get confused but this was very confusing. I

got out of bed and wandered
about. Now this is also *very*
unusual because if there's one
thing I don't do it's wander
about in the middle of the night
– well, you never know what
you're going to meet, do you?
Especially around here . . .
Well, the next thing that
happened was . . .
A noise.
Terrifying . . . awful . . .
Out of this world. Look, I'm not
easily frightened . . . but this . . .
cor . . .

In DOUGAL'*s dream an owl's voice was heard
saying ''Allo, cheeky!'*

Well then I thought – perhaps
I'm dreaming , because who ever
heard of an owl speaking?
But then I heard something else
. . . a voice.

'I wish to serve the blue voice. I
wish to be the blue king. I wish
to be all powerful . . .'

And then I heard another voice.

'Blue is beautiful
Blue is best
I'm blue
I'm beautiful
I'm best.'

Well, the voices were coming
from the old factory on the hill –
you know, the one where they
used to make treacle. It's been
empty for years but *now* it had
lights on.
Well, being as you know, a
brave spirit, I thought I'd get a
better look at it all – so moving
backwards to confuse anyone
with evil intents into thinking I
was going forwards, I got myself
with some cunning into a
position of vantage.
What did I see, you will ask?
Not very much, I answer.
(*Quickish*) The old factory was
there on top of the hill but
everything seemed craggy and
very sinister and *very blue*.
And then I heard the voice
again.

'Blue is beautiful

Blue is best
I'm blue
I'm beautiful
I'm best.'

All this talk about *blue*. Very
funny. I've never been very fond
of blue meself, not with my
colouring.
So I wandered back to my little
bed and I put myself back to
sleep . . . And if you can make
anything of *that* you're very
welcome to try. And the best of
luck.

ZEBEDEE *asked* DOUGAL *if he was sure he hadn't
been dreaming.*

DOUGAL: What? Of course I'm sure! I
                 don't imagine voices in the
                 middle of the night. Well, not
                 often.

ZEBEDEE: Then all I can say is . . .

DOUGAL: Yes? Yes?

ZEBEDEE: . . . that I haven't the slightest
                 idea what it all means.

DOUGAL: Oh.

ZEBEDEE: And I suggest you ask Florence.
                She may be able to help. She's a
                very sensible girl, you know.

DOUGAL: Er, Zebedee, you don't think I
                ought to see a psychiatrist, do
                you?

ZEBEDEE: Don't be silly, Dougal.

DOUGAL: You don't think I'm going dotty,
                do you?
                Do you?

ZEBEDEE *bounced off across the garden.*

                He didn't answer!
                He didn't answer!
                I'll go and see Florence. She's
                painfully well adjusted.

FLORENCE *was singing at home and singing a
song which went something like this:*

FLORENCE: Florence, it's a lovely morning
                Florence, shall you work this
                morning?
                Florence, if you don't this

morning
You will never do it, dear!

Florence, you would rather
wander
Florence, it's a living wonder
That your house is not now
under
A great big cloud of dust, dust,
dust.
Clean it up you must, must,
must.

Mirror, mirror on the wall
Who's the fairest one of all?
Not that you should care at all
Being fair's not worth a jot
Be content with what you've got
What you've got is quite a lot.

Florence, it's a lovely morning
Florence, shall you work this
morning?
Florence, if you don't this
morning
You will never do it, dear!
Florence, will you come back
here?
There's none so deaf as will not
hear

Now she's gone for good, I fear!

Florence met Mr Rusty and the
others.
Hallo, how are you? they all
said.
We're glad you're come . . . they
all said.
Because we've . . .
got . . .
a surprise . . .
they all said.

FLORENCE: Oh, I love surprises more than
              anything. What is it?

Look on the roundabout, said MR RUSTY. Look
on the roundabout and you'll see.

So FLORENCE looked on the roundabout. She
looked again . . . She got a bit closer and she saw
. . . a cat.

FLORENCE: Oh, how beautiful!

CAT: Yes.

MR RUSTY: First blue cat I've ever seen.

The CAT stretched and got up.

CAT:	Call me Buxton.
MR RUSTY:	Oooh! It speaks. I thought perhaps it was stuffed.
FLORENCE:	Buxton . . .

The BLUE CAT *began to dance. Everyone cheered.* ZEBEDEE *arrived to see what was happening.*

FLORENCE:	We've got a beautiful visitor. A blue cat. A beautiful blue cat . . . called Buxton.
MR RUSTY:	Never seen one before.
ZEBEDEE:	Er . . . Dougal's got a bit of a problem he wants to talk to you about.
FLORENCE:	A problem?
ZEBEDEE:	That's what he told me – a problem.

But no one really wanted to know about DOUGAL *and his problems. They had a blue cat and couldn't think of anything else.*

MR RUSTY:	It's not a day for problems . . .

it's a day for celebration and
delight.

MR RUSTY *turned the magic roundabout. The*
BLUE CAT *laughed slyly to itself.*

CAT: Oh, this lot's going to be a
                    pushover. A pushover!

I'd better have a word with DOUGAL, *I suppose,*
said FLORENCE.

DOUGAL *was picking flowers.*

DOUGAL: Constance Spray strikes again
                    . . .
                    I'll leave these here for Florence
                    and give them to her later.
                    Now, I wonder where she is.

FLORENCE *heard* DOUGAL *coming and told the*
BLUE CAT *to hide. 'You're a surprise,' she said.*

FLORENCE: (*Bright*) Hallo, Dougal!

DOUGAL: Oh? You seem revoltingly bright.
                    How are you? Well? What's the
                    matter? Cat got your tongue?

FLORENCE: Funny you should say that,
                    Dougal . . .

FLORENCE *stroked* DOUGAL's *head.*

DOUGAL: Oh bliss! Bliss! Do it again!
Thank you . . .
Oh, I've got something for you.
Wait there. Won't be long.

The BLUE CAT *was watching.*

CAT: 'Allo! We've got a right one 'ere.

DOUGAL *brought* FLORENCE *the bunch of flowers
he had picked.*

DOUGAL: Just a little something. I picked
them myself. Sweets to the sweet,
you might say. What a lovely
turn of phrase.

FLORENCE: Oh, Dougal, they're lovely.
Thank you very much. I'll put
them in water later.

DOUGAL: It's nothing. Er . . . you weren't
foolish enough to bring *me*
anything, were you? Lump of
sugar, perhaps? Or two lumps?

FLORENCE: Look behind you, Dougal.

DOUGAL *saw the* BLUE CAT, *screamed and ran away.*

Isn't he lovely?

DOUGAL: What *is* it? *What is it?*

FLORENCE: Can't you see, Dougal? It's a cat – a beautiful blue cat called Buxton.

DOUGAL: Buxton?

FLORENCE: Yes, he's come to visit.

DOUGAL: Buxton!!

The BLUE CAT *came over to meet* DOUGAL.

CAT: Aye, that's the name, lad. Buxton.

DOUGAL: Er . . . pleased to . . . er . . . how are you?

CAT: Very well, ta.

DOUGAL: Good.

CAT: Thank you.

The BLUE CAT *gazed around the garden.*

> (*Slow*) You've got a lovely place here. I'm very very taken with it. Yes, it's very lovely. Grand.

FLORENCE: Yes, well, we like it, don't we, Dougal? And, er, we're glad you like it too. Aren't we, Dougal.

DOUGAL: Oh, ecstatic. We're overcome with delight. Absolutely overcome.

CAT: In that case, I take it there'd be no objection to my staying – *indefinitely?*

DOUGAL: Indefinitely? Ah . . . Oh . . . Ah . . . I – I don't think you'd like it that much. It . . . er . . . rains a lot, doesn't it? And you'd get wet, and I'm sure you'd hate that. Ha! Ha! There's a train at three. Goodbye.

FLO: (*Whisper*) Don't take any notice of Dougal.

CAT: No, I won't.

24

	You know, it's very kind of you to ask me to stay.
DOUGAL:	Not at all . . . (*Aside*) A cat, of all things! And blue! Oh dear.
CAT:	I find it funny you haven't remarked on my colour. I'm blue, you know. Blue.
DOUGAL:	Oh yes! Yes, you are! Yes, you are blue, aren't you?

The only blue cat in the world, said FLORENCE.

DOUGAL:	Yes, well, there aren't many yellow dogs called Dougal, but I suppose that doesn't matter any more . . . Fickle jade.

The news of the arrival of the BLUE CAT *had spread around the magic garden and everyone arrived to have a look and to say hallo.* DYLAN, ERMINTRUDE *and* BRIAN.

BRIAN:	Oooh yes! You are blue, aren't you? *Very blue.*

CAT:	And what might this lad's name be?
FLORENCE:	Oh, that's Brian.
CAT:	Funny name for a snail, isn't it?
DOUGAL:	Ooooooh! Look who's talking. Blue Buxton.
ERMINTRUDE:	Oooh . . . blue is beautiful.

That reminds me, said DOUGAL. *I heard some very funny voices coming from the old factory last night.*

From the old factory? they all said. But it's closed.

CAT:	(*Sharp*) Factory? Did you say factory? What do you know about the factory . . . eh? What's all this about the factory, eh? eh? Factory?
DOUGAL:	Well, don't go on. I just heard voices in the old treacle factory, that's all.

No one was very interested in DOUGAL *and his*

voices but they were interested to know where
BUXTON *was going to stay.*

CAT: Oh, don't worry about me. I'll
        find a little niche somewhere.

Everyone seemed to think that the most perfect
niche would be DOUGAL's *house. It wasn't very*
far away, and as BRIAN *said,* DOUGAL *had plenty*
of room – and a great big bed.

DOUGAL: Now wait a moment. Wait a
           jolly moment, you lot.

CAT: Thanks very much. It's very kind
        of you to offer. I accept. Which
        way is it?

DOUGAL: I didn't offer! I didn't offer! He
           can't stay in my bed. Where will
           I sleep? What will people say?
           What?

Have a good rest, said FLORENCE.
I'll try, said BUXTON.

They all set off for DOUGAL's *house.*

Nearly there, said BRIAN. *Oh, you'll love it here.*
It's very elegant and chic.

CUCKOO: (*Camp*) Please be *quiet* – I'm trying to get some sleep!

Ignoring this, DYLAN *started to play a little welcoming lullaby for* BUXTON *while* ERMINTRUDE *and* BRIAN *made up the bed.*

DYLAN: In this life, little cat
There are few pleasures that
Give the same lift
Have the same gift
As getting into a big soft bed.
(Forgive me, man, if I just say
that I would rather it me than
you in the hay . . .)

CAT: Oh, that looks comfy. Ta.
I shall sleep like a baby – don't
bother to wait.

The BLUE CAT *climbed into* DOUGAL'S *bed and settled down for a snooze.*

Thank you, and good night.

BRIAN: Well, that's got him safely
tucked up.

ERMINTRUDE: Doesn't he look *sweet*? And so
blue. We're very lucky to have

such a distinguished visitor. Oh
my, yes!
Come along, darlings.

The CUCKOO *hung up the clock pendulum for a*
soothing tick tock.

Meanwhile, FLORENCE *was picking some blue*
flowers and wondering where the BLUE CAT *had*
come from.
Suddenly the colour blue seemed to be very
important to her and she wondered about that,
too.
Why was it? she thought. Blue. Why blue?
DOUGAL *was wondering about the colour blue*
too.

DOUGAL: Blue cats, indeed! It's against
                nature. It'll be blue snails next,
                and then where will we be? Blue
                snails!

DOUGAL *left the others to it. He wandered off to*
the old factory. Suddenly he trod on to an old
hoist and was lifted high up off the ground. He
was stuck, but had a splendid view of the
surrounding area.

DOUGAL: Help! Help!

The blue CAT *sat up in* DOUGAL's *bed.*

CAT:

Did I hear a noise? No, all's well. Now for the factory and my master plan.
Sleep on, little rabbit. Now's the time for me to take over this place and everyone in it.
Oooh, I'm so wicked. Soon I'll be king of this garden . . . if I can only pass the test.

DOUGAL:

Who put this thing here? The positions I find myself in. Really! Ssshh! Someone's coming. Oooh, that cat. He mustn't see me. I'll never live it down.

CAT:

(*Fast*) No one about – good. No one must see me – especially that nosy dog Dougal. He might get suspicious.

DOUGAL:

(*Whispering*) I'm suspicious already . . . Oh good, he can't see me. Now what's he doing, the blue rotter?

The BLUE CAT *stopped at the old factory gates.*

CAT:	Open up! Open up! I've arrived to claim my rights!
VOICE:	Who are you?
CAT:	Oh, the blue voice!
VOICE:	Who are you?
CAT:	The cat – Buxton.
VOICE:	Ah, the cat. The blue cat?
CAT:	(*Rising*) The *same*. At your service, madam. Ready to claim my rightful kingdom. Ready to serve the blue cause. Ready to carry the blue flag, ready to be true blue... Ready to wipe out all other colours. Like heliotrope!
VOICE:	That's enough, Buxton dear. There'll be time for drama later. Are you ready for the test?
CAT:	Ready, madam.
VOICE:	Well, remember. If you fail . . . Enter, blue cat, and claim your kingdom. If you can.

Remember there are seven doors
before you get the crown.
And remember, there is no going
back . . .

The gates shut behind the BLUE CAT.

For instance, look behind you.

CAT: 'Eh up!

A crossbow bolt struck the wall only inches from
BUXTON's *head.*

VOICE: Just a little warning, Buxton.
                Now, what is the colour of the
                first door?

CAT: (*Whisper*) Blue?

VOICE: Well done, Buxton. You have
                your first title. You are now a
                knight.

The gate swung open.

                Come in, Sir Buxton. Now, what
                do you think I'm doing here?

CAT: Oh madam, you are clever. You

are making flowers. Blue
flowers.

VOICE: (*Builds up*) Correct, Sir Buxton.
We are making blue flowers.
Soon the world will forget the
primrose. Flowers are blue! All
others must go!
Blue is beautiful
Blue is best
I'm blue
I'm beautiful
I'm best.
(*Very loud*) What is the colour
of the second door?

CAT: Cobalt blue!
Am I right?!!

VOICE: Right again, *Baron* Buxton.

*The second door opened to the sound of
trumpets. The* BLUE CAT *gazed around.*

CAT: (*Whisper*) What's this?

VOICE: This, Baron Buxton, is where we
dye the clothes of the world.
Blue is the only colour to be
worn. Down with the shades of

red and green. Down with the colours of the day. Deadly nightshade is our game. Down with fun clothes – horrid things. Down with shades of pink and grey. Down with everything but blue!
(*Slow*) Down with Debenham and Freebody's . . .
The third door!

CAT: The door to the room of dreams?

VOICE: But what colour?!

CAT: Er . . . Saxony blue!

VOICE: Right! *Lord* Buxton!

The third door opened to reveal a room full of masks, terrifying and sinister.

CAT: Ooh 'eck!

MASK WITH EYES: How you feeling, little Buxton?

OTHER MASK: How's your luck, Buxton . . . ton . . . ton . . .

GRIMACING MASK:
(*Slow*) Enjoying yourself, Buxton?

ANOTHER MASK: Frightened, Buxton? Frightened?

CAT: Eee . . . eck! Where's the door?

VOICE: (*Shouts*) The colour?

CAT: (*Shouts*) Indigo!!

VOICE: Go through, *Marquis* Buxton. (*Slow*) This is the room of the world. The blue of the oceans, the blue of the skies. The sun never rises on the colour blue. Even the stars will be blue . . . even the stars. (*Loud*) What is the colour of the fifth door?

CAT: Oh 'eck . . . eee . . . aah . . . I've forgotten.

The crossbow moved into position.

Nay, nay, I'll remember! I'll remember!

VOICE:	(*Menace rising*) Remember quickly, Marquis Buxton. Remember quickly or pay the price of the blues in the night! Rememberrrrrr . . .
CAT:	I've remembered! Baby blue!
VOICE:	Well remembered, *Duke* Buxton.
CAT:	The room of thunder and lightning! The room of anger and rage!
VOICE:	Right, Duke Buxton! And the next door?
CAT:	Prussian blue. Am I right?
VOICE:	(*Whisper*) Well done, *Prince* Buxton.
CAT:	The guard room, I presume.
VOICE:	Correct, Prince. This is the room where your army is made. The army that will enable you to take over the garden and

everything in it. With these
soldiers you will be invincible.
Nothing will be able to stand in
your way. Nothing! You will be
all-powerful, all-knowing . . .
for always. You will be king . . .
king . . . king . . .

The machines began to churn out a BLUE ARMY.

Now, show me how the cat
jumps!

CAT: The last door! The door of the
blue king. *Royal blue!*

VOICE: Success, King Buxton!

CAT: I've done it! I've done it! King
Buxton . . . the First!

The CAT *entered the throne room, guarded by his*
BLUE ARMY.

Ee . . . 'eck!

I am king of everything that I
survey,
I am king and no one here can
say me nay.

I am king, the bluest king in all
the world.
All the world, even Bognor and
Crewe.

I am king and everyone had best
watch out.
I am king and liable to throw a
clout
At anyone who gets across my
path.
Cross my path, even armies and
you.

I am king and everything I do is
bad.
I am king, the wickedest you've
ever had.
I am king, and anything that
doesn't please
Gets the chop or gets thrown in
the stew.

SOLDIERS: He's the king, the wickedest one
We've ever had.
He's the king, the bluest one
We've ever had.
He's the king, the cattiest one
We've ever had.
He's the king, he's the king,
He's the king.

The CAT *played on a blue piano, a virtuoso with tail and paws. One of the soldiers began to dance and sing, but was shushed by its fellows.*

CAT: I'm the king, by cleverness I got the job.
          I'm the king, I've every right to thump and rob,
          I'm the king and everything that's red or green,
          Will be dyed, even pansies and rue.

          I'm the king, it's tiring but rewarding work.
          I'm the king, my duties I will never shirk.
          I'm the king, my reign of terror's just begun,
          So watch out if you're not painted blue.
          Soldiers: Encore!

CAT: Right, you lot. This is the first command of your king – that is *me*, King Buxton!
          Everything not blue, unless it belongs to me, will be destroyed!
          Everyone not blue will be taken prisoner and chucked in the dungeons.

SOLDIERS:	(*Crescendo*) Taken prisoner – we obey
	Totally destroyed – we obey
	Taken prisoner – we obey
	Totally destroyed – we obey.
	We go, we go, we go,
	To thump, pillage and burn.
	We go, we go, we go,
	We'll give people aturn.
	Our king is the best.
	We go, we go, we go.
CAT:	Good lads. Total war on colour.
	Let battle . . . commence!
SOLDIERS:	(*Six times*) We go, we go, we go.
CAT:	Well, go on then! Go!

Meanwhile, back at DOUGAL's *place,* BRIAN *and* FLORENCE *wondered where the* BLUE CAT *had got to. He wasn't in* DOUGAL's *bed.* DYLAN, *the guardian, was still asleep and* DOUGAL *himself was nowhere to be seen.*
It's all a bit of a mystery, said BRIAN.

| BRIAN: | Do you think they've gone off somewhere together? |

FLORENCE: I don't think that's very likely,
              Brian. But you go and see if you
              can find Dougal. All right?

BRIAN: Yes, all right.

FLORENCE: And I'll see if I can find Buxton.
              I don't suppose they've gone
              very far.
              Goodbye.

BRIAN: That dog always goes too
              far . . .

ERMINTRUDE *was painting*.

ERMINTRUDE: Oh, how beautiful. What a
              lovely example of my blue
              period.
              (*To Brian*) Hallo, dear creature.

BRIAN: Oooh! It's a bit blue, isn't it?
              What is it?

ERMINTRUDE: It's abstract.
              (*Sings*) I'm in the mood for blue.

BRIAN: You never told me you could
              paint.

ERMINTRUDE: Well, you never asked me, dear thing, did you?
The muse came upon me – like it does – and I felt blue. I'm painting these for dear Buxton.

BRIAN: Dear Buxton's disappeared. Gone without trace.

ERMINTRUDE: Disappeared without trace? Just when he'd come into my life?
Oh, I must lose myself in my art.

In the meantime, DOUGAL *was still stuck up on his hoist.*

DOUGAL: Oh dear, it must be way past teatime . . .
Oh, someone's coming.
Help! Help!

BRIAN: Do I hear sounds of distress:

DOUGAL: Help! I'm up here!

BRIAN: I'm sure I heard a voice . . .

DOUGAL: Look up, you great clump!

BRIAN: Sounds like my lovely shaggy

chum, but I'm sure he wouldn't call me a great clump . . . no, he *wouldn't*, not *him*.

DOUGAL: Oh dear, it would have to be him. Great oaf!

BRIAN: Oh, someone's left a rope across the path – that's very dangerous.

BRIAN *began to chew through the rope holding* DOUGAL'*s hoist aloft.*

DOUGAL: Don't do that!
Oh! Oh! Oh!

BRIAN: Did I hear a noise of falling? No, couldn't have. Eugh! Got a mouthful of rope . . . Now I wonder where old shaggy breeks has got to.

DOUGAL: If I stay I'll do that snail an injury. Really . . . I'm lumbered. And that cat. He's up to no good in the old factory and they're all dotty about him. (*Shouts*) Great fools! Blind fools!

FLORENCE: Dougal, whatever's the matter?

DYLAN:	Like . . . what's wrong, man?
DOUGAL:	I wish I knew.
ERMINTRUDE:	Trouble, dear hearts?
FLORENCE:	Well, Dougal seems upset about something.
DOUGAL:	I have every reason to be upset. That cat's up to no good.
BRIAN:	I've been looking for you, old matey. I thought I heard you calling just Now. You sounded to be in distress, but I expect I imagined it. (*Whisper*) What's up with him?
GROUP:	(*Whisper*) We don't know.
DOUGAL:	Friends, Romans, Countrymen!
FLORENCE:	I beg your pardon, Dougal?
DOUGAL:	We have a traitor in our midst. It's that blue cat. I saw him go into the old factory, and I know in my bones that he's hatching

some fiendish plot against our beloved garden.

Now I don't know what it is, but we have got to be very careful, all of us. NATO must be alerted. The United Nations should be told. The Security Council must be roused. I might even write to *The Times*, if I can find a stamp.

BRIAN: (*Whisper*) He's dotty!

DYLAN: (*Whisper*) It had to happen, man.

DOUGAL: Don't just stand there. Unite! Pull yourselves together. We must man the barricades. We must even *dog* the barricades. We must prepare – for war!

ERMINTRUDE: Well, I'm prepared, dear heart. I've been prepared for years. I was in the Land Army.

DOUGAL: Yes, well, I'm sure your experience will be invaluable, madam, but be that as it may, we must prepare to defend our garden. We must be on our guard. Has anyone got an anti-cat fence?

The BLUE CAT *appeared behind some rocks, but stayed hidden.*

We have a traitor in our midst. I mean, a cat amongst our pigeons. A bull in our china shop. We have a viper in our bosom. We have a snake in our grass. A dog in our manger . . . what am I saying?

CAT: Hum, I shall have to act quickly. That dog suspects something. I shall need to cunningly reassue them and make him feel small. Hallo . . . each.
Something wrong?

FLORENCE: *(Whisper)* No . . .

CAT: Having trouble?

GROUP: *(Whispers)* No . . . no . . .

DOUGAL: Yes! We're having trouble with the blues – especially blue cats!

The BLUE CAT *pretended to cry.*

CAT: Oh dear, oh dear. Once more
                my colour has been rejected. I
                thought here I would be happy –
                amongst my new friends.
                Oh woe . . . woe . . . woe . . .

BRIAN: Very moving.

DYLAN: Sure is, man.

DOUGAL: He'd do well at the Old Vic, that
                one.

FLORENCE: Hush, Dougal!

And they all assured the BLUE CAT *that they did
trust him and they wanted him to stay.*

ERMINTRUDE: I've even done some paintings
                for you, dear blue thing, which
                I'd like you to come and see. I've
                done them in my new blue style.

CAT: Oh, I'm touched! I'm overcome
                with touch. Thank you.

DOUGAL: (*Hiss*) Don't be deceived!
                Don't be taken in!

That cat is a menace!
That cat is dangerous!
That cat is a cat!

FLORENCE: Oh Dougal, you are dreadful.

DOUGAL: Oooooh! Blind fools!

The CAT *admired* ERMINTRUDE's *paintings.*
DOUGAL *followed him.*

CAT: Oh, great!

DOUGAL: May I have a word with you,
cat?

CAT: Later, dog.

DYLAN: Like, dramatic moments, man.

BRIAN: Oh, he's a great one for drama,
is Dougal.

MR MACHENRY *and* MR RUSTY *arrived, rather
disturbed about something.*

Strange things were happening,
they said.

CAT: What sort of things, friend?

MACHENRY/RUSTY:
    Difficult to explain.
    There's been a rash of blue
    cactuses.

DOUGAL: See? Trouble!

RUSTY: Great prickly things they are –
    and blue.
    Eek! There's another.

A blue cactus popped out of the ground.

MACHENRY: I've never seen anything like it.
    I've never seen anything like that
    at all.

CAT: Oh, I have.
    Oh yes, it's the fast-growing
    variety. What a beauty!

ZEBEDEE: Help! Help!

They heard ZEBEDEE *calling. Something dreadful
had happened. He had lost his magic moustache.
Someone had stolen it from beside his bed.
Without it he had no magic – he was powerless.
It was a tragedy.*

CAT: Oh, what a tragedy. How very
    unfortunate for your friend.

ZEBEDEE: Stop chattering! Help me find it. Please!!

FLORENCE: Yes, we must all help find it.

They all went out into the garden to look for the magic moustache. All except the BLUE CAT.

DOUGAL: It's going to be tears before bedtime. I know.

CAT: (*Aside*) Oh, I'm so evil. Now that I've got his moustache, nothing can stand in my way. I must launch – my attack!

DOUGAL: Oh dear, without his moustache he's useless. And I've got a feeling we're going to need him. Oh dear.

BRIAN: Moustache! Moustache! Where are you, little creature? Come on . . . come out . . .

The BLUE CAT *returned to the old factory.*

CAT: The hour has come . . . Open for the king! Crown!

The crown descended gently on to his head.

<blockquote>
Thanks very much.
Time to attack!
</blockquote>

SOLDIERS: Time to attack!
                         Time to attack!
                         Time to attack!

CAT: Good lads.

SOLDIER: Time to attack!

CAT: Shut up!

In the old factory everyone was preparing for war.

MASKS: Bad dreams!
                         Nightmares!
                         Time to attack!
                         Get ready!
                         Carry on!

THUNDER ROOM: Thunder and lightning!
                         Storms and tempests!
                         Time to attack!
                         Carry on!

OTHER ROOM: The time is ripe.

Everything is ready.
Time to attack!
Carry on!

SOLDIERS: We go, we go, we go,
We go, we go, we go,
We go, we go, we go,
We go . . .

CAT: Shut up!
(*Soft*) Please, shut up . . .
Right, you horrible lot. You
know what to do, don't you?
Everyone is to be taken prisoner.
No one must escape. Or heaven
help the lot of you!
Carry on!

SOLDIERS: We go, we go, we go,
To thump, pillage and burn
We go, we go, we go,
We'll give people a turn.
Our king is the best,
We go, we go, we go,

We go, we go, we go,
Let nowt challenge our might.
We go, we go, we go,
To turn day into night.
Our king is a cat,
We go, we go, we go.

The SOLDIERS *marched out of the old factory and into the garden. The* CAT *watched them through an old periscope.*

CAT:	Right, periscope. Let's look up!
CAPTAIN:	Company . . . 'alt! By the right! Wait for it. By the right – attack!

One by one the friends were all taken prisoner by the ghostly BLUE SOLDIERS. *All except* DOUGAL.

ERMINTRUDE:	Oooh! Who are you? What do you think you're doing? Let go of me, cheeky thing. Oh, I'll give you such a piece of my mind in a moment. Really. I've never been so insulted in all my life! Oooh!
FLORENCE:	Help! Help! Zebedee!
DYLAN:	Peace, men, peace!
CAT:	You'll be lucky! Ah! A triumph! All captured. The dreaded cactus everywhere. A triumph! Wait a mo! Where's that dog?

Curses and black pudding! They haven't got that dog! I'll 'ave their guts for garters, you see if I don't.

Meanwhile, DOUGAL *had found a* SCARECROW *wearing a luxuriant moustache.*

DOUGAL: Er, excuse me, sir, is that *your* moustache?

SCARECROW: (Posh) It certainly is – so go away.
Oh, why aren't you with the others? They're all captured, you know.

DOUGAL: Captured?

SCARECROW: Yes, captured. They were all carried orf by some dashed soldiery. They were shoutin' and screamin' dreadfully. Not at all British. In fact I found the whole thing distinctly unfresh.

DOUGAL: Where did they go? Did you see?

SCARECROW: Yes, they took them to that old factory on the hill.

DOUGAL *scampered around in a frenzy of anxiety.*

> Oh, he's gorn. Funny the people you meet nowadays. Wouldn't have done when I was in the Guards. We'd have shown them, by Jingo!

DOUGAL *came back to the* SCARECROW.

DOUGAL: Captured and taken to the old factory . . . Are you sure?

SCARECROW: Do you mind? There's some funny things happening around here, too. Me lettuces have all turned blue.

DOUGAL: Oh, the fiend! He wants to make everyone sick with blue salad. The fiend! The fiend!
The factory, you say? I shall go and rescue them!

SCARECROW: Yes, well. Best of luck, old chap. I'd let you have a lettuce, but property *is* sacred.
Funny chap. Needs a good haircut, by George.

Everywhere was devastation. DOUGAL *didn't
know what to do.
He was determined to rescue everyone, but how?
He was alone. All alone.
Back at the old factory the* BLUE CAT *was gloating
over his prisoners.*

CAT: Oh, I'm so evil. All my plans are
        working out. Soon I will be
        master of the whole garden –
        and then you'd all better watch
        out.
        How are you all, by the way?
        (*Fast*) Not too comfortable, I
        trust? Perhaps you're missing
        your little shaggy friend Dougal?
        Well, I'll get him soon – don't
        you fret.

FLORENCE: (*Pleads*) Tell us it's a game,
        Buxton.

ZEBEDEE: Oh, if only I had my moustache.

CAT: Your moustache! (*Laughs*)
        Pardon my mirth but you'll
        never see that again. I've got it.

A lightning flash illuminated the BLUE CAT
wearing ZEBEDEE'*s moustache.*

BRIAN: You're a rotter!

RUSTY: What you going to do with us
            now?

DYLAN: Could I trouble you men to . . .
            like not rattle your chains so
            much? I'd like to get a little sleep
            here.

CAT: Make the most of it, my little
            rabbit. Make the most of it.
            You'll never get out of this
            place.

As the BLUE CAT *spoke, stalagmites and stalactites
came shooting of the floor and ceiling all around
them, creating an impenetrable barrier.*

*The stalactites and the stalagmites will keep you
here for ever! For ever!*

ERMINTRUDE: And to think I wasted my artistic
            talent on him! It's not fair.

RUSTY: Don't cry, don't cry. Dougal will
            rescue us, you'll see.

CAT: Dougal? Oh, pardon again my
            evil mirth, but that dog couldn't

get in here in a million years.
For one thing, he's yellow!
Eugh!!
You have to be blue to get in
here. And that means *me* – the
greatest.
Me – King Buxton the First. *Me!*

VOICE: Don't forget *me,* Cat.

CAT: Oh no, madam. No, madam.
Certainly not, madam.

VOICE: Good. I wouldn't like you to get
ideas above your station – until
you have completed everything I
require to be done.

CAT: Your servant, madam.

VOICE: I hope so.

CAT: (*Whisper*) But not for long.
You'll go the same way as the
others, *madam*. When I am
master – *madam*.

Back in the garden, DOUGAL *filled a tub with blue
dye and jumped in.*

DOUGAL: Right, if you've got to be blue to get in . . . I'll be blue. Ooooh. Looks quite nice.

He made his way back to the factory gates.

Hmmm. Looks a bit prickly. Now what do we have to do to get in here? Er, open sesame? No, not very likely, I suppose. There must be some way innnnnnnnn!!!

He dropped through a hidden trap door, right into the throne room and was soon surrounded by guards.

Oh! Oh! Er . . . . (*Scots*) Er . . . I just dropped in. I hope I'm not intruding? Er . . . is this the Co-op?

CAT: (To the guards) As you were! And who are you?

DOUGAL: Me? Oh, I'm . . . er, Peter. Er, Blue Peter, but you can call me Bluey.

As he looked around he saw something lying in a cabinet by the throne.

(*Aside*) Zebedee's moustache! Lovely day!

CAT: Why 'ave you come?

DOUGAL: *Well* – you're famous, aren't you?

CAT: Yes, you could put it like that. Stand back, he's a friend.

DOUGAL: So I said to myself, I must go and see the famous Blue King and pay my respects. It's the least you can do, Dou- er Peter, I said. Pay your respects. So I'm paying them.

CAT: You remind me of someone.

DOUGAL: Oh, I know. Isn't it a bore? I've often been told that I look like that splendid – I mean stupid - dog Dougal who lives around here somewhere. It's really most trying. After all, we're entirely different. I'm blue

	– and he's always eating sugar, foolish animal – and I can't *abide* sugar.
CAT:	Is that a fact? Guards! Surround him!
DOUGAL:	Eh? What? What? What? Stop! I'm your friend!
CAT:	Take him to the torture chamber. If he *is* Dougal he won't be able to resist the torture. Oh, I'm so *evil*.

DOUGAL *found himself in a strange room full of sugar, and he realised this was the fiendish torture arranged by the* BLUE CAT. *If he ate any of the sugar the* CAT *would know he was* DOUGAL *and all would be lost. If he didn't eat any, the* CAT *would believe he was Blue Peter – the blue dog.*

	What a fiend! But what was he to do? The sugar was very tempting . . . Even granulated.
DOUGAL:	Oh, it's too much.

What am I going to do? I don't
think I an stand it. Ooooh, I'd
make a rotten spy.

To eat or not to eat – that is the
question. Whether tis nobler in
the stomach to suffer-

Oh, shut up, Dougal! If you eat
one lump you're lost. You must
get out of here . . . now . . . and
fast.

Go on, run! Run! Oh . . .
locked. Locked in a room with
fourteen tonnes of sugar. Surely I
could have *one* lump?

No!

Yes?

No!

Yeees?

Oh! The torture! Oh!

Come on, pull yourself together,
Dougal. Be a dog! Remember
you're British! Remember your
friends.

Rescue them first and eat the
sugar later.

Hey! Your majesty!

Your majesty. Why have I been
put in this room with all this love
– er revolting – sugar. Let me
out. I feel quite sick. Quite sick.

CAT:	Interesting! He didn't eat any. So he can't be Dougal. Come out, my dear friend. You've passed the test safely. You realise, I had to be absolutely sure. I can't take any chances in my position.
DOUGAL:	Say no more about it, your majesty. In your position you can't be too careful. (*Aside*) The rotter!
CAT:	Come in, dear friend. Come in. Don't stand on ceremony. Just bow low. Thank you. (*Fast*) I want everyone to know that this is my Prime Minister!
ALL:	Long live the Prime Minister! Long live the Prime Minister!

DOUGAL *walked proudly down the red carpet in front of the throne, covertly looking around for his friends.*

DOUGAL:	Too kind.
CAT:	You're looking for something, PM?

DOUGAL: Just making sure there are no
                 spies about. You can't be too
                 careful. Er . . . which way are
                 the dungeons?

CAT: I'll show you. They're very
                 interesting.

DOUGAL: (*Fast*) No, no, don't you bother.
                 I'm sure you must be very busy.

CAT: That's true. I have many things
                 to do, being King.

SOLDIERS: Long live the King! Long live the
                 Prime Minister!

DOUGAL: Well, let's hope so . . .

In the dungeons FLORENCE *sang a sad song . . .
something like this:*

FLORENCE: This game is not a good game,
                 I can't believe it's happening,
                 It must be all a dream.

                 This game is not like my game,
                 I'm in the dark and frightened,
                 I'm in the dark and lonely,
                 It must be all a dream.

Shall we ever see the sun again?
Shall we ever see the rain again?
Shall we ever play our games
again?
Or will the games we play end
here?

Oh Dougal, where are you?
I'm sorry, Dougal, I'm sorry.
It's all my fault, but I
Thought everything was all
Right – like it usually is,
It's all my fault.

Somehow I know it's my fault
I should have trusted no one
My trusting spoiled the game.

Next time I'll be more careful,
Next time I'll look behind me,
Next time I won't be foolish,
Next time will be all right.

Shall we ever see the sun again?
Shall we ever see the rain again?
Shall we ever play our games
again?
Or will the games we play end
here?

All the friends were crying now, tears pouring down their cheeks. The outlook was bleak.

I'm sorry, Mr Rusty. But I do feel rather sad.

RUSTY: Don't worry. I'm sure everything will be all right. And I'm not often wrong about these things.

FLORENCE: I'll try, but it does seem a bit hopeless . . . doesn't it.

DOUGAL *came into the dungeons.*

DOUGAL: Yoo hoo!
Yoo hoo!
Anybody there? It's me . . . you know? Where are you, you soppy lot?

FLORENCE: Dougal! Is that really you?

DOUGAL: (*Whisper loud*) Of course it's me! But don't call me Dougal. I may have been followed. Call me Peter – or just be quiet.

CAT: Are you there, Prime Minister, dear?

DOUGAL: Here, your majesty.
Just having a look round.

The others realised DOUGAL *had a plan.*

CAT: Met my prisoners, have you!

DOUGAL: Yes, what a pathetic lot!
Ya! Sucks! Boo!

BRIAN: And the same to you, blue bag!

ERMINTRUDE: Blue – bag!

BRIAN: Blue – bag! Stinky-poo!

ERMINTRUDE: Blue – bag!

CAT: Don't you dare mock my Prime
Minister.

ZEBEDEE: Prime Minister? Don't make me
laugh.

CAT: Silence, little springing fool!
We are blue!
My friend and I are blue-oo-oo!

DOUGAL *and the* BLUE CAT *sang a duet and
danced the tango.*

DOUGAL:	We're blue, we're blue, etc
CAT:	My friend and I, my friend and I, to one another true-oo.
DOUGAL:	We're true, we're true, we're true.
CAT:	We have a yearning to be evil.
DOUGAL:	We may be mad, we may be bad, but most of all we're evil.
CAT:	He speaks the truth, the lovely lad, but I am worse than he is!
DOUGAL:	Yes he is worse, it's true he's worse He makes me look quite good . . . 'ood – 'ood – 'ood – 'ood – 'ood – Ole!
CAT:	Do you come here often?
DOUGAL:	Yes he is worse, yes he is worse. He makes me look quite good.

DOUGAL *and the* BLUE CAT *became separated by a blue wall.*

CAT: Hey, something appears to have come between us.

DOUGAL: My friend the king, my friend the king, let nothing come between us.
No, no, no, no, no, no, no, Ole!

VOICE: (*Silky*) I'm glad you're enjoying yourselves . . .

DOUGAL: Who's that?

CAT: Madame Blue.

DOUGAL: Oh yes! Oh, oh yes! She sounds lovely.

VOICE: And what is *your* name, dog?

DOUGAL: Oh, I'm Prime Minister – Peter.

CAT: *My* Prime Minister – Blue Peter.

VOICE: (*Slowish*) Good. You will need all the help you can get to further the next stage of my plan in the conquest of the Universe.
Listen, and listen carefully.
You are going to the moon!

DOUGAL *and the* BLUE CAT *exchanged anxious glances.*

> You have volunteered, haven't you?

The BLUE GUARDS *surrounded the pair of them.*

CAT: I think we've volunteered, your majesty.

VOICE: (*Ecstasy*) I want the moon for my blue kingdom!
Blue moon, you are the one . . .
Bon voyage!

CAT: Oh! I wish I knew where that dog Dougal was . . .

DOUGAL: (Aside) Oooh, I was all set to rescue them, now Madame sends me to the moon. The things I do!

The guards escorted him to the space rocket.

> All right! All right! All right! Really!

Lights flashed and the rocket doors shut.

I'm not sure I like this.

The rocket moved into launch position.

5! 4! 3! 2! 1!

Lift off.

DOUGAL: Oh dear! Oh dear!

The rocket landed on the moon. DOUGAL *jumped out first.*

Hallo, moon. Anybody about?
Ah well, one small step for a dog
but a great step for dogkind.
What a lovely turn of phrase. I
must remember to write it down
when I get back. If I get back.

CAT: I claim this moon for me – King
Buxton . . . . . . the First.
What a place. Worse than
Barnsley. It's lak of water that
does it.
(*Fast*) Lack of water! Aaagghh!

DOUGAL: Suddenly I feel thirsty.

At that very moment DOUGAL *fell into a water-filled crater.*

Aaarrgh! There's no lack of
water down here! Get me out!

CAT: Oh – a major discovery. Hang
on, Prime Minister.

DOUGAL *emerged from the crater. Disaster!
Unbeknownst to him all the blue dye had been
washed out of his fur.*

DOUGAL: Oh! Oh! Oh! I thought you said
there wasn't any water?
I'll catch me death! Atchoo!

CAT: Bless you.
(*Fast*) You're not blue . . .

DOUGAL: What are you taking about, your
majesty . . . Sir?

CAT: (*Hiss*) Dougal!

DOUGAL: No, I'm Peter. Blue Peter.
Remember? Peter . . . your
chum. Peter.

CAT: Come back here!

DOUGAL: Oh, the water's washed my dye
off! What shall I do?

The BLUE CAT *chased* DOUGAL *around the moon
and finally into the rocket. The rocket took off
for Earth, spinning out of control. At last the*
BLUE CAT *threw* DOUGAL *out of the rocket.
Luckily,* DOUGAL *had a parachute and landed
safely by the old factory.*

DOUGAL: Worried were you?

The BLUE CAT *was feeling space sick.*

CAT: Oh! Oh! Oh! I feel really poorly!

VOICE: Cat? Back already?

CAT: My Prime Minister – it's Dougal
                 the dog!

VOICE: (*Rising*) So you've failed!
                 You know the penalty for
                 failure.

CAT: Please, let me explain.

VOICE: No, I will not let you explain.
                 You are no longer King! You are
                 nothing! Out of my sight before I
                 lose my temper. And when I lose
                 my temper there's *TROUBLE!
                 TROUBLE! TROUBLE!*

*Thunder and lightning bolts hit the old factory
and it began to fall apart.* DOUGAL *hurried to
rescue his friends from the dungeon, undoing their
chains.*

FLORENCE: Dougal! Dougal!

DOUGAL: Quick! Run! Run!
                Don't stop! Hurry up, you lot!

BRIAN *stopped at the old factory gates.*

BRIAN: We've forgotten something . . .
                We've forgotten something, old
                mate.
                Have *you* got it?

DOUGAL: Hurry up, rabbit!

VOICE: Failed! Failed!
                All my dreams of a blue universe
                have failed.
                Blue is beautiful
                Blue is best
                I'm blue
                I'm beautiful
                I'm best . . .

*Finally the throne room collapsed and the whole
factory fell in.*

And that was that!

DOUGAL: Fun while it lasted. Oooh, you're looking a little pale.

FLORENCE: Oh, Dougal – thank you very much.

She stroked DOUGAL's *head.*

DOUGAL: Oh bliss! Bliss!

FLORENCE: Oh look!
It's Buxton!
He's crying.

DOUGAL: He's got something to cry about, the rotter!

FLORENCE: Oh Dougal . . . no. It's very sad!

CAT: How can you ever forgive me? I've been a beast.

RUSTY: Yes, you have been a bit of a beast – but we forgive you.

CAT: You're all too good to me – too good.

ERMINTRUDE: Oh! Where's Brian? He's not here? I can't see him anywhere.

FLORENCE: Yes, where is he, Dougal?

DOUGAL: Oh, I remember. He went back into the factory.

ERMINTRUDE: Oh Dougal, he didn't – did he?

DOUGAL: (*Crying*) He said he wanted to fetch something. I expect it was his lettuce.

RUSTY: Oh, poor Brian. Poor Brian.

DOUGAL: My best friend . . . We had our ups and downs but – *sniff*!

MACHENRY: (*Irish*) He used to help me in the garden . . .

ERMINTRUDE: I can't stand it!

RUSTY: He was so, so . . . jolly.

FLORENCE: What will we do without him?

DOUGAL: See what you've done, cat!

CAT: Yes, it's all my fault. All my
                fault. I'm evil, I know.

DOUGAL: You should *blush* for shame.

CAT: Oh yes!

The CAT *blushed red, then white, then red, then
white again. When he finished blushing he was no
longer blue but white, with only a hint of blue
around his ears and paws.*

                Forgive me, each. I was the
                victim of a false doctrine. I am
                now changed. May I be your
                friend? Your true friend?

BRIAN: Oh that's so moving! Oh, I'm
                quite overcome.
                Hey, we must forgive him, you
                lot!

DOUGAL: Snail? Where have you been.
                You've had us all very very
                worried.

BRIAN: Have you missed me? It's just
                that I realised we'd forgotten
                something so I took my little self
                back to get it. And here it is.
                Ha! Ha!

BRIAN *showed them* ZEBEDEE'S *moustache, rescued from the old fatory.*

ZEBEDEE *was beside himself with joy. His magic was back again.*

DOUGAL: Right, who's for a cup of tea.

MACHENRY: Tea can wait. Look what's over here . . . Look what's over here – and it's not blue. In fact, I think it might be very white soon.

The magic roundabout had appeared, and soon the roundabout and the magic garden were covered in snow.

RUSTY: I think you've overdone it, but, ALL ABOARD!

ERMINTRUDE: Oh I love snow.

ERMINTRUDE *turned in excited circles, then fell into a snow drift.*

CAT: I'll bet she feels a bit blue, eh?

DOUGAL: Yes, yes, I'll bet she does. What? What!

Blue, indeed. DOUGAL *chased the* CAT *through the snow. It was no laughing matter.*

MR RUSTY *turned the handle of the magic roundabout, so they all got on the roundabout and sang a song which went something like this:*

> Now the colour game is done
> Now we know it wasn't true
> Now the colours all have won
> Now we're anything but blue
>
> No adventure should be in vain
> May we all meet together again
>
> How can it matter where you
> live
> Live where you like they're
> always there
> Magic thoughts can always give
> Magic gardens everywhere.

THE END

Eric Thompson was born on November 9, 1929 in Sleaford, Lincolnshire and brought up in the village of Rudgwick in Sussex.

He trained to be an actor at the London Old Vic School and joined the company in 1952 where he met his wife, the actress Phyllida Law. Their daughters, Emma and Sophie are both actors.

A founder member of the Royal Exchange theatre in Manchester he directed several plays there and in the West End of London, Washington, Broadway, Holland, New Zealand and Canada.

He first wrote the *Magic Roundabout* from his cottage in Argyll where he hoped to retire with a clinker built boat, a soft-topped jeep and a collie dog. He died in 1982.